Big Brown Bear

David McPhail

Green Light Readers
Harcourt, Inc.
Orlando Austin New York San Diego Toronto London

Bear is big.

Bear is brown.

Bear goes up.

He comes down.

Bear gets paint.
The paint is blue.

Bear goes up.
The paint goes, too.

Little Bear is playing.
She has a bat.

Oh no! Little Bear!
Do not do that!

Bear *was* up.
Bear comes down.

Bear is big. . . .
But he's *not* brown!

Bear washes up.
He's brown once more.

He washes the windows,
then the door.

Bear gets more paint.
It's green, not blue.

Bear goes up.
The paint goes, too.

Bear is painting.
He's all set.

But look out, Bear!

It's not over yet!

In the story, Bear went up and Bear went down. Sing this song about something else Bear might do!

Bear went over the mountain.
Bear went over the mountain.
Bear went over the mountain.
To see what he could see!

Sing-Along!

Meet the Author-Illustrator

Many of David McPhail's books have bears in them. He likes to draw bears. They remind him of Teddy, the bear he had when he was a child. Teddy would go with him everywhere.

David McPhail doesn't have Teddy anymore, but he has another big toy bear in his office that keeps him company.

Who keeps you company?

David McPhail

www.HarcourtBooks.com

First Green Light Readers edition 1999
Green Light Readers is a trademark of Harcourt, Inc., registered in the
United States of America and/or other jurisdictions.

The Library of Congress has cataloged an earlier edition as follows:
McPhail, David M.
Big brown bear/David McPhail.
p. cm.
"Green Light Readers."
Summary: A big brown bear turns blue with paint when a little bear
accidentally knocks over his ladder with her baseball bat.
[1. Bears—Fiction. 2. House painting—Fiction.] I. Title.
PZ7.M478816Bi 1999
[E]—dc21 98-15568
ISBN 0-15-204817-0
ISBN 0-15-204858-8 (pb)

A C E G H F D B
A C E G H F D B (pb)

Ages 4-6

Grade: 1

Guided Reading Level: G

Reading Recovery Level: 10-12

Green Light Readers
For the reader who's ready to GO!

"A must-have for any family with a beginning reader."—*Boston Sunday Herald*

"You can't go wrong with adding several copies of these terrific books to your beginning-to-read collection."—*School Library Journal*

"A winner for the beginner."—*Booklist*

Five Tips to Help Your Child Become a Great Reader

1. Get involved. Reading aloud to and with your child is just as important as encouraging your child to read independently.

2. Be curious. Ask questions about what your child is reading.

3. Make reading fun. Allow your child to pick books on subjects that interest her or him.

4. Words are everywhere—not just in books. Practice reading signs, packages, and cereal boxes with your child.

5. Set a good example. Make sure your child sees YOU reading.

Why Green Light Readers Is the Best Series for Your New Reader

• Created exclusively for beginning readers by some of the biggest and brightest names in children's books

• Reinforces the reading skills your child is learning in school

• Encourages children to read—and finish—books by themselves

• Offers extra enrichment through fun, age-appropriate activities unique to each story

• Incorporates characteristics of the Reading Recovery program used by educators

• Developed with Harcourt School Publishers and credentialed educational consultants